A Valentine's
Surprise

READ ALL THE CANDY FAIRIES BOOKS!

Chocolate Dreams

Rainbow Swirl

Caramel Moon

Cool Mint

Magic Hearts

Gooey Goblins

The Sugar Ball

COMING SOON:

Bubble Gum Rescue

Double Dip

Candy Fairies

A Valentine's Surprise

HELEN PERELMAN

ILLUSTRATED BY
ERICA-JANE WATERS

ALADDIN
NEW YORK   LONDON   TORONTO   SYDNEY   NEW DELHI

ALADDIN

An imprint of Simon & Schuster Children's Publishing Division

1230 Avenue of the Americas, New York, NY 10020

First Aladdin paperback edition December 2011

Text copyright © 2011 by Helen Perelman Bernstein

Illustrations copyright © 2011 by Erica-Jane Waters

All rights reserved, including the right of reproduction in whole or in part in any form.

ALADDIN is a trademark of Simon & Schuster, Inc., and related logo is a registered trademark of Simon & Schuster, Inc.

For information about special discounts for bulk purchases, please contact Simon & Schuster Special Sales at 1-866-506-1949 or business@simonandschuster.com.

The Simon & Schuster Speakers Bureau can bring authors to your live event.

For more information or to book an event contact the Simon & Schuster Speakers Bureau at 1-866-248-3049 or visit our website at www.simonspeakers.com.

Designed by Karina Granda

The text of this book was set in Berthold Baskerville Book.

Manufactured in the United States of America 0814 OFF

6 8 10 9 7

Library of Congress Control Number 2011920262

ISBN 978-1-4424-2215-5

ISBN 978-1-4424-2216-2 (eBook)

For Sarah Collier, a sweet and true fan

Contents

Supersweet Surprise

Raina the Gummy Fairy sprinkled handfuls of colorful flavor flakes into Gummy Lake. She smiled as the gummy fish swam over and gobbled up the food. Watching the fish eat made Raina's tummy rumble. She had gotten up very early and had been working in Gummy Forest all morning. When she settled on a perch high up on a gummy tree, Raina opened her back-pack. All the animals in the forest were fed, and now she could relax and eat her own lunch.

Raina had an important job in Sugar Valley. She took care of the gummy animals that lived in Gummy Forest. There were many types of gummy animals, from friendly bear cubs to playful bunnies. Raina was fair and kind to each of the animals—and they all loved her.

"Hi, Raina!" a voice called out.

Raina looked up to see Dash, a Mint Fairy, flying in circles above her head. The small, sweet fairy glided down to see her.

"I was hoping to find you here," Dash said. "I need your help."

Raina was always willing to help out any

of her friends. She had a heart that was pure sugar. "What's going on?" she asked.

Dash landed on the branch next to Raina. She peered over at the bowl in Raina's hand. Dash was small, but she always had a huge appetite!

"Hmmm, that smells good," she said. "What is that?"

"It's fruit nectar. Berry brought me some yesterday," Raina told her. She watched Dash's eyes grow wider. It wasn't hard to tell that Dash would love a taste. "Do you want to try some?" she asked.

"Thanks," Dash said, licking her lips. "Berry's nectars are always supersweet." Dash leaned over for her taste. Berry the Fruit Fairy had a flair for the fabulous. And she could whip up

4

a spectacular nectar. "Yum," Dash continued. "Berry makes the best fruit nectar soup."

Raina laughed. "I don't think I've ever heard you say that you didn't like something a Candy Fairy made," she told her minty friend.

"Very funny," Dash said, knowing that her friend was speaking the truth.

"Have you come up with any ideas about what to get Berry?" Raina asked.

Dash flapped her wings. "That is why I'm coming to see you," she said. "I was hoping you could give me an idea. I know Berry would love something from Meringue Island, but that is a little too far. She's the only one I haven't gotten a gift for, and Valentine's Day is tomorrow. Since it's also her birthday, I want to make sure the gift is supersweet."

"Sure as sugar, Berry would love anything from Meringue Island," Raina agreed. Meringue Island was in the Vanilla Sea and was *the* place for fashion. Berry loved fashion—especially jewelry and fancy clothes. When Fruli, a Fruit Fairy, had come to Sugar Valley from the island, Berry was very jealous of her. Fruli had beautiful clothes and knew how to put together high-fashion looks.

"The truth is," Raina added, leaning in closer to Dash. "Berry would like anything you gave her."

"But I want to give her something she is really going to love," Dash replied. She swung her legs back and forth. "I want to surprise her with a special gift this year." Her silver wings flapped quickly. "I wish I could think of something with extra sugar!"

"I know how you feel," Raina said. "I've had

the hardest time coming up with an idea." She looked over at Dash. "I'll tell you what I'm going to get her, but please keep it a secret."

"Sure as sugar!" Dash exclaimed. She clapped her hands. "Oh, what are you planning?"

Raina took her last sip of the fruit nectar. "Last night I was reading a story in the Fairy Code Book, and I got a delicious idea."

Dash rolled her eyes. "I should have guessed that this would have something to do with the Fairy Code Book," she said.

Raina read the Fairy Code Book so often that her friends teased her that she knew the whole book by heart.

"Well," Raina continued, "there is a great story in the book about Lyra, the Fruit Chew Meadow unicorn."

"Oh, I love Lyra," Dash sang out. "She grows those gorgeous candy flowers at the edge of the meadow." Just as she said those words, Dash knew why Raina's grin was so wide. "You talked to Lyra, and she is going to give you a special flower for Berry?"

Raina laughed. "Dash!" she said. "You ruined my surprise." She put her empty bowl back inside her bag. "I thought that if I got Berry a flower, I could make a headband for her. You know how she loves to accessorize."

"The more the better, for Berry," Dash added. "And those are the fanciest flowers in the kingdom. *So mint!* Berry is going to love that headband." Dash stopped talking for a moment to take in the whole idea. "Wait, how'd you get

Lyra to do that for you? Unicorns don't like to talk to anyone!"

Raina smiled. "Well, that's not really true," she said.

"Let me guess," Dash said. "Did you read that in a book?"

Raina giggled. "Actually, I didn't," she told her friend. "To be honest, I think Lyra is just shy."

"Really?" Dash asked. "Can I meet her? Maybe she'll have another idea for a gift for Berry. Let's go now." She stood up and leaped off the branch into the air.

"I've been working all morning," Raina said. She reached her arms up into a wide stretch. "Maybe we can go in a little while?"

Dash fluttered back down to the branch. Her

small silver wings flapped quickly. "Come on," she begged. "Let's go now!"

Dash was known for being fast on the slopes of the Frosted Mountains—and for being impatient. She liked to move quickly and make fast decisions.

Leaning back on the gummy tree, Raina closed her eyes. "Please just let me rest a little, and then we can go," she said with a yawn.

"All right," Dash said. "Do you have any more of that nectar?"

Raina gave Dash her bowl and poured out some more of Berry's nectar. Then she shut her eyes. Before Raina drifted off to sleep, she imagined Berry's happy face when she saw her birthday present. Sure as sugar, Valentine's Day was going to be supersweet!

CHAPTER

2

Sweet Lyra

After Raina woke up from her nap, she and
Dash flew to Fruit Chew Meadow. The meadow
was on the other side of Candy Castle and wasn't
that far away from Gummy Forest. Raina knew
that with Dash, the trip would go fast. Dash
was a champion at sledding and loved to fly
down the slopes of the Frosted Mountains and

Marshmallow Marsh on her sled. Raina usually preferred to take her time. She liked to see the colorful sights of Sugar Valley and enjoy all the delicious scents blowing in the breeze. Today, however, she was ready to race Dash to Fruit Chew Meadow.

"I can't believe I'm keeping up with you," Raina called over to Dash.

Dash smiled. "I'm glad you *are* going fast. I can't wait to talk to Lyra!"

Laughing, Raina shook her head. Her minty friend always wanted a speedy answer. Raina flapped her wings. She was excited to see the flower that Lyra had for her.

"I thought unicorns were a little sticky when it came to being around fairies," Dash said.

"Not Lyra," Raina said. "She's not like that

at all. Besides, Lyra likes Berry very much. She wants to help make her birthday special."

"Berry is going to be so happy!" Dash said, smiling.

Now that Candy Castle was behind them, Fruit Chew Meadow was just ahead. The fairies flapped their wings faster and giggled as they headed toward the ground. As they drew closer, Raina stopped laughing and squinted her eyes. Normally, the far end of Fruit Chew Meadow was full of flowers. The bright rainbow of colorful flowers was always such a breathtaking sight. But today the field looked different.

"Oh no!" Raina gasped. Her wings slowed as she glided above the meadow. Usually, the tall candy flowers were reaching up to the sky, but now they were dragging on the ground.

"Holy peppermint," Dash mumbled as she flew closer to the field. "These flowers look awful."

"What happened?" Raina said. She hovered above the ground, staring at the sad-looking flowers. "This must have just happened. We would have heard of this for sure."

"Sour news travels fast," Dash agreed. "I'm sure Princess Lolli doesn't even know about this, otherwise she would be here now."

Princess Lolli was the fairy princess who ruled over Sugar Valley. She was fair and true and always helped out the fairies when there was trouble.

"I wonder if anyone else knows about this," Dash said. She spun around. "Do you see Lyra anywhere?"

Raina held her hand over her eyes to shield the sun. She scanned the meadow. "I don't see her. We have to find her." She flapped her wings and flew up to see better. "Lyra's usually right here near the berry cherry tree," she said. "I wonder where she could be." She looked over at Dash.

"I don't have a good feeling about this," Dash said. She wrinkled her nose. "Something smells sour here."

"Well," Raina said, trying to stay calm. "Let's look for clues. That's always the best way to solve a mystery."

The two fairies hovered above the meadow and searched.

"Poor Lyra," Dash said. "This must have happened after all the Fruit Fairies left this morning."

Raina nodded. "You must be right," she said. "The Fruit Fairies would have helped. Keep looking!"

As Raina flew over the meadow she wasn't sure what she was looking for. Lyra was a large white unicorn with a rainbow horn that glowed. There weren't many places for an animal that size to hide in the meadow.

"Wait!" Raina said. She flew down to the ground and squatted low on the grass. Dash followed close behind her.

"Lyra's hoofprints!" Raina exclaimed. She pointed to a dirt path and a small hoofprint. "If we follow these, maybe we can find her."

The two fairies followed the hoofprint clues. Near the edge of the meadow they found the unicorn.

"Oh, Lyra!" Raina cried out. She saw the beautiful white unicorn lying down behind a berry thistle and rushed toward her.

Lyra was lying on her side. Her normally bright rainbow horn was dull and nearly wiped of color.

Raina sat by Lyra's head and stroked her nose. "Lyra, are you okay?" she whispered softly in her ear.

There was no answer.

"Lyra," Raina begged. "Please answer me. What happened?"

Dash sat down on the other side of Lyra's head. She rubbed her silky white neck. "Lyra, can you hear us?" she asked.

Lyra's eyes fluttered slightly.

"She looks very weak," Dash added. "Poor

Lyra!" She bent down to get a closer look at the unicorn. "She's really sick."

Raina knew they had to do something—and fast. It was hard to tell just how long Lyra had been lying there. And her dull horn was very upsetting. "We need all of us together to solve this problem," she said.

Lyra's eyes fluttered again. The unicorn's long lashes seemed too heavy to let her keep her eyes open.

"It's all right," Raina told her. She patted Lyra gently. "We're going to get you some help," she whispered in her ear.

"And try to figure out what went on here," Dash added.

Raina stood up and looked around. The field seemed so strange without the tall stalks of colorful flowers. "Maybe she hurt herself," she said softly. She looked over Lyra's white body, but the unicorn appeared unharmed.

"We can't move her by ourselves," Dash said. Lyra was a full-sized unicorn and much too large for just two Candy Fairies to pick up.

Raina knew Dash was right. "Let's send sugar flies to our friends. If we're all together, we can come up with a plan."

The fastest way to get information around Sugar Valley was to send a sugar fly note. Those little flies could spread news faster than anyone.

Poor, sweet Lyra, Raina thought. *How did this happen to you?*

Raina touched the unicorn's horn and closed her eyes. She wished she could help the gentle creature and find out what had made her so sick.

 20

CHAPTER 3

A Sour Mystery

Raina and Dash sat by Lyra's side. The unicorn seemed to be resting, but she was weak and her horn was still dull. Raina didn't like seeing the unicorn so sick.

"Let's try to make Lyra more comfortable," Raina said. She gathered some soft fruit chews and put them under Lyra's head. "Oh, I hope the others get here soon!" she said, looking up at the sky.

"Let's tell everyone that we were working on a special candy for Princess Lolli," Dash said. "I don't want to give away Berry's surprise gift. She'll figure out that we were up to something."

"Maybe," Raina said. "But then there will be questions about the special candy." She reached over and pet Lyra. She felt very warm. "Telling one little lie doesn't seem bad, but one lie always leads to many, many more."

Dash agreed. "You're right. We'll just say that we came to see Lyra. Everyone will be thinking about how to help her."

Putting her head close to Lyra's nose, Raina listened carefully. "She's barely breathing," she told Dash.

"Look!" Dash cried. "I see Melli and Cocoa!"

Up in the sky the Caramel Fairy and Chocolate Fairy were headed toward them. Raina waved. Just as they landed Berry flew in beside them.

"Sour strawberries!" Berry exclaimed. "What happened here?" She bent down to Lyra. "I was just here this morning and Lyra was fine. Oh, the poor thing." Gently she stroked the sleeping unicorn's neck.

"Sweet Lyra," Melli sighed.

"She doesn't look well," Cocoa added. She glanced around at all the wilted flowers in the meadow. "Melli and I were nearby around lunchtime, and the flowers were standing tall. So Lyra couldn't have been lying here for long."

"Oh, Lyra," Berry cooed. She sat down close

to her. "Sour sugars! Look at her horn!" Berry looked at Raina. "Her magic!"

"We have to get her some help," Raina said. She was trying very hard to remain calm.

"Unicorns hold all their magic in their horn," Berry blurted out. "Lyra must be very sick if her horn is so dull."

Raina lowered her eyes. She was aware of that fact, but she had been too worried to say those words out loud.

Melli paced around Lyra. "Oh, this is awful. And a mystery."

"A sour mystery," Dash mumbled.

Cocoa flew up in the air and scanned the meadow. "All of Lyra's flowers are drooping. Whatever is affecting her is affecting the whole meadow."

"The flowers respond to Lyra," Berry said. "If she doesn't have her magic and she can't sing, the flowers will die." Berry's wings began to move. "We have to do something fast."

Raina put her hand on Berry's shoulder. "That is why we called you all here."

"Let me stay with Lyra," Berry said. She reached in her bag for some fruit nectar. "Maybe she'll have some." She held the food out to the unicorn, but there was no movement.

"She's so weak," Melli said sadly.

Raina's eyes were brimming with tears. She knew that she had to be strong. "Berry, you stay with Lyra and keep her calm. The rest of us will search the meadow. We'll look for clues."

The fairies all agreed. Berry stayed with Lyra as Raina, Dash, Melli, and Cocoa flew back and forth over the meadow. Overall, the meadow didn't look disturbed . . . except for the wilted flowers.

"Holy peppermint!" Dash cried out. She waved her friends over to the edge of the meadow. She zoomed down to the ground and then signaled her friends to follow.

"A broken fence!" Raina exclaimed. She landed beside Dash, the others right behind her.

The thick caramel fence surrounding one of the flower beds was broken.

"Those fences are incredibly strong," Melli said. She bent down to examine the break. "That caramel is hard to crack."

Cocoa ducked down low to get a better view. "Well, something—or someone—broke the fence."

Dash sat down on the ground and put her head in her hands. As she stared at the broken fence her nose began to twitch. She put her hand on the ground and then up to her mouth. "Holy peppermint!" she said softly. "There's salt all over the ground here." She stood up and began to follow the path while the others watched her with puzzled expressions. Suddenly Dash bent down, scooped something up in her hand, and then she showed it to her friends.

"Salt?" Melli asked. "How could there be salt here? Everyone knows . . ."

Before she could finish her sentence, her friends were around her. Melli had her hand in front of her mouth. She couldn't bear to say the words.

"Salt is poisonous for unicorns!" Raina blurted out.

"Mogu! That salty old troll," Cocoa hissed.

"No wonder Lyra is weak and sick," Melli said softly.

Dash was so angry her wings flapped and took her up off the ground. "Mogu has been coming to the meadow to steal candy! And his salty tracks have harmed Lyra. This is so sour— even for Mogu."

"You really think Mogu would hurt Lyra?" Raina asked. "Even for a troll that would be superbitter."

"Maybe he didn't realize the salt was harmful to Lyra," Melli offered.

"Not likely," Cocoa muttered. "He saw a broken fence as an invitation."

"Sweet sugar," Raina gasped. "We need to get Lyra stronger so that she can sing and get back to guarding the meadow." She looked at her friends. "And we need to tell Berry. She's not going to handle this well."

"And Berry's birthday is tomorrow," Melli added sadly. "This doesn't seem like a time for celebrating at all."

Raina took a deep breath. "Dash and I came here to get one of Lyra's flowers so we could make Berry's birthday gift extra-sweet." Raina looked over at Fruit Chew Meadow and sighed. "We still have time to solve this mystery and to make Berry's birthday *and* Valentine's Day special." She looked at the worried expressions on her friends' faces. "We have to at least try."

CHAPTER 4

A Salty Problem

When the four friends returned to the far end of Fruit Chew Meadow, Berry was still sitting next to Lyra. The unicorn had not moved since they had left. Berry was stroking Lyra's neck and singing softly.

"Gentle breeze and sweet light," Berry sang out,

"flavors of the rainbow grow bright . . ."

"How is Lyra?" Raina asked, kneeling beside her friend. The white unicorn was still asleep and her horn was still dull. Not a trace was visible of the colors that normally glowed from her horn. "Did she wake up?"

"Yes, she took a few sips of the nectar but then dozed off again," Berry said. "Did you find any clues?"

Raina decided not to sugarcoat the truth. "We found a broken fence and a trail of salt," she told her.

"Salt?!" Berry exclaimed. Her eyes were wide and full of concern.

Raina knew that Berry was aware of the dangers of salt in the meadow.

"Oh, this is worse than we thought," Berry said softly. She looked into Raina's eyes. "It's Mogu, isn't it?"

"We're not sure," Raina told Berry. "But the first thing we need to do is get rid of the salt. If we can clear the area, maybe Lyra will be able to speak to us and tell us what happened."

"Let's try to wash all the flowers off," Berry said.

Raina smiled at her Fruit Fairy friend. "That's what I thought too. We'll make a spring rain to take the salt away. We can go to Red Licorice Lake for the water."

"I'll stay with Lyra," Berry offered. She looked down at the gentle unicorn. "She seems to do better when I sing to her."

Raina gave her friend a quick hug. "That is a great idea," she said. "You stay here."

The four fairies flew down to the shores of Red Licorice Lake. They each grabbed a bucket from a nearby shed. Buckets were kept there in case of droughts or other emergencies.

This is definitely an emergency, thought Raina.

"Once the salt is gone, Lyra will feel better, right?" Dash asked Raina as she filled up her bucket.

"I hope so," Raina replied. She didn't know for sure, but she knew that the salt was causing Lyra to grow weak and sick. "Come, let's hurry," she urged her friends.

Together, the fairies flew up and down the meadow. They poured the water over the wilted

flowers and washed the white salt away. With each trip to the lake, the salt was slowly disappearing. It took many trips and bucketfuls of water, but soon the wet meadow didn't have a trace of salt.

Then the fairies gathered back around Lyra and Berry.

"How is Lyra?" Raina asked as they flew up.

"She's a little better," Berry told her. "Getting rid of the salt has helped. I can see she's a little stronger."

"This still doesn't make sense to me," Raina said. She sat down next to Berry, tapping her finger to her head. "Mogu is afraid of Lyra. Why would he even come here?"

"Who would be afraid of a sweet unicorn?" Dash asked.

"When it comes to Mogu, there isn't always a solid reason," Berry told her.

"I remember those tall stalks of salty pretzels in Black Licorice Swamp," Cocoa told her friends. "If there is salt here, I'm sure it's because of Mogu and the Chuchies."

Raina knew that Cocoa was remembering the time when she flew to Black Licorice Swamp. Mogu and his mischievous companions, the Chuchies, had stolen her chocolate eggs. Cocoa had tricked Mogu into giving them back. The Chocolate Fairy knew all about the troll's salty ways.

"If there is salt here, Mogu is probably to blame," Cocoa said again. "His greed will drive him to do anything." Thinking of her chocolate eggs made Cocoa stamp her foot. "We have to trick Mogu again," she said. "Cleaning up the meadow may solve the problem for now, but that troll will be back."

"Especially if Lyra isn't guarding the flowers," Melli added. "There's nothing here to stop him."

"We're here now," Raina said bravely. "It's sticky business to trick a troll," she reminded her friends. She reached into her bag. "I know I've heard a story about Mogu and Lyra. Maybe there's a clue in a story that can help us."

Raina took out her Fairy Code Book and thumbed through the pages.

Dash sat down next to her. "I can't imagine Mogu being afraid of anything."

Flipping through the book, Raina agreed. "Yes, yes, I'm sure I've read a story in here about Mogu and Lyra. I think it was about Lyra's pointy horn."

Laughing, Berry slapped her hand to her knee. "I bet that horn can come in handy when dealing with Mogu," she said, giggling.

"What is the story?" Dash asked. She was growing impatient.

"Mogu was once pricked by Lyra's horn when he tried to steal her fruit-chew flowers," Raina read from the thick book. She turned the book around to show her friends the picture. "I knew there was a story!"

"Ha!" Dash burst out. "Look at that!" She pointed to a picture of Mogu with a tear in his pants. Sticking out of the hole was Mogu's polka-dotted underwear. "No wonder Mogu is afraid of Lyra. She totally embarrassed him!"

"You should really read the Fairy Code Book more often," Raina scolded her friends.

"We don't have to," Berry said, smiling. "We have you! You remember every story."

Melli put her arm around Raina. "And it's a good thing, too," she said. "Raina, what would we do without you?"

Blushing, Raina turned the page. "This was many years ago, and Mogu has not been back here since. I wonder what made him come back now."

"Maybe he just wanted to have a fruit-chew flower," Berry offered. "They are the sweetest in Sugar Valley."

Raina looked over at Dash. She didn't want her to say anything about the gift for Berry. She caught Dash's eye. Dash immediately understood and bit her lip. It was hard for Dash not to speak her mind!

"Or maybe he heard about the broken fence

and thought he could slip in unnoticed," Dash said.

"Who knows why a salty old troll does anything," Melli said. She got up and paced around in a circle.

Berry rubbed Lyra's dull horn. "Lyra needs help," she said. "Cleaning the meadow is not going to wash this problem away."

Raina hugged the Fairy Code Book close to her chest. Normally, reading a story helped her decide the right thing to do. But this tale offered little advice. All she knew for sure was that Lyra was not better. Berry was right, just washing the meadow wasn't going to solve the problem. If they were going to help Lyra, they had to come up with a plan to stop Mogu. And to get Lyra well again.

And that was a salty problem she had no idea how to solve.

CHAPTER
5

Burst of Hope

Raina and Berry huddled together on a blanket in Fruit Chew Meadow. Normally, Raina would have loved to spend time hanging out with Berry. Only now they were both worried about Lyra. Lyra had been resting under Berry's pink cotton-candy shawl, but she still looked very weak. The others had flown off to get some food for dinner. Raina was having a hard time keeping still. Her wings were fluttering and she was twisting her long hair around her finger.

"You're worried about Lyra, aren't you?" Berry asked.

"Yes," Raina said. But she couldn't tell Berry that Lyra was not all she was concerned about. She also didn't want to ruin Berry's birthday with this sour event. With the look of things now, it didn't seem that Lyra would be getting better by Sun Dip. Normally, Sun Dip was a festive time of day when fairies would gather. The sun would slide behind the Frosted Mountains and the sky would turn deep pinks and purples. Fairies would share sweet treats and talk with friends. But today when the sun went down, there'd be little Raina and her friends would want to celebrate.

Raina touched the Fairy Code Book in her bag. She wished the story about Mogu and Lyra had helped her come up with a plan. She sighed.

"Mogu has a way of ruining sweet times in Sugar Valley," Berry said softly. She leaned forward to pet Lyra. "Please, Lyra, take some nectar. It will make your throat feel better. We all need you to sing."

Raina blew her bangs off her forehead. Lyra was not getting stronger, even though all the salt had been washed away. They were going to have to move her. "How are we going to move a unicorn?" Raina asked.

"We've brought food," Cocoa called from above.

"I'm not really hungry," Raina replied.

"Me neither," Berry told Cocoa.

Cocoa, Melli, and Dash came to sit on the blanket. They spread out the food for their friends.

"We should eat," Melli said. "Then we can think of a solid plan."

Dash looked around at the pale, wilted flowers. "What do you think will happen to the flowers if Lyra's voice doesn't come back?" she asked.

Raina lowered her head. "I'm not sure," she said. "I don't think the flowers will survive. Already they look even less colorful, and it's only been a few hours."

"The greatest present for my birthday would be if Lyra would get better," Berry mumbled.

Hoping that she could make her friend's wish come true, Raina gave Berry a tight squeeze.

"We still have time," she said, trying to believe her words would come true.

A gentle breeze ruffled the grass. Above them Raina spotted a sweet sight. "Oh, Berry!" she cried out. "It's Princess Lolli!"

In a flash, Princess Lolli was standing before them. Her long strawberry-blond hair hung down at her shoulders, and a small candy-jeweled tiara sat on top of her head. She smoothed her bright pink dress with her hands and smiled at the young fairies. "Hello, fairies," she said. "I heard that Lyra is not well. I am so glad you are here with her."

"I don't think we've helped her much," Berry said sadly. "She is still very weak."

"Lyra can't sing," Raina said, stepping forward. "We found a broken fence and salt. We washed

the flowers and tried to get Lyra to drink some nectar. Nothing seems to be working."

"Salt?" Princess Lolli said. Her smile melted into a frown. "I was afraid that was the case."

"Do you think Mogu was here?" Cocoa asked.

"I'm not sure," the princess said. "I do know that Lyra needs some help. Let's get her to Candy Castle."

Raina bent down low to Lyra. "She can't even open her eyes. She's so weak," she said. "Lyra can't fly. How can we get her to Candy Castle?"

Everyone looked at one another.

"Bitter mint," Dash mumbled. "This is a super minty problem. Without Lyra's glowing horn, she can't fly. She's out of the race."

"That's it!" Raina shouted. Her wings flapped happily, and she rushed over to give Dash a hug.

"What?" Dash gasped.

Raina grinned at her friend. "I know exactly what we need to do," she told her friends. "I'm sure this will work!"

For the first time since they had arrived at Fruit Chew Meadow, Raina suddenly had a burst of hope.

6

Sweet and Strong

Raina was grinning while her friends gazed at her. Their mouths were open and their eyes wide.

"You really think that will work?" Cocoa asked.

Melli bit her lower lip. "Sweet caramel, Raina," she muttered. "I'm not sure we could pull that off."

"Sure as sugar, we can!" Raina exclaimed. She stood up straight, with her hands on her hips. "We have Dash, the best sled racer in Sugar Valley. We'll make a sled mint enough for a sweet unicorn. If Lyra can't fly, we'll have to pull her to Candy Castle."

Princess Lolli smiled. "Raina, that is an excellent idea," she said. "If there are any fairies who can make this happen, I believe those fairies are right here in front of me now."

"What about Mogu?" Dash asked. "What if he comes back?"

"We'll have to wait to deal with Mogu," Princess Lolli told the fairies. "First we must help Lyra." She bent down to the unicorn and whispered in her ear. Lyra slowly opened her eyes. Princess Lolli took a pink sugar cube from her

pocket and held it out to Lyra. The unicorn took the sweet treat and then closed her eyes again. Standing up, Princess Lolli faced the fairies. "I will head back to the castle to make arrangements for Lyra. I will see you all shortly."

The fairies waved good-bye to Princess Lolli. They were so thankful that she had come, but now they had work to do! If they were going to build a sled big enough for a unicorn, they had to work quickly.

Raina opened the Fairy Code Book. She put the book down on the ground for everyone to see. "Look, there's a picture of a large sled," she said. "This sled was for Mooco the chocolate cow, when she was stuck in the terrible winter storm last year in Chocolate Woods." She held up the book to show her friends the illustration.

"Hot chocolate!" Cocoa shouted. "I remember that storm. That poor cow was stuck in the thick frozen chocolate. It took every Chocolate Fairy's help to get her out."

"I think we can use this picture of a large sled to help us," Raina said. "If the Chocolate Fairies could move Mooco, we can move Lyra." She turned to Dash. "What do you think? Can we make a sled big enough for Lyra?"

Dash leaned over to see the picture. "Sure as sugar," she replied. She smiled at Raina. "Just as Princess Lolli said, we are the fairies for the job!"

Raina was thankful for the Mint Fairy's enthusiasm. She knew she could always count on Dash.

"We'll need a few supplies," Dash said. She started to pace back and forth as she thought out loud. "We'll need some fruit leather, red licorice, and something to hold the sled together."

"What about hot caramel?" Melli asked. "When the sticky syrup dries, it should hold the sled together."

"Thanks, Melli. I think you're right," Dash said. "The hot caramel is a smart choice."

Berry leaped up. "I can get the fruit leather," she said. "We'll need wide strips, and I know where to get good, strong pieces."

"I can get the licorice," Cocoa offered.

"I'll head to the Frosted Mountains to get the frosting for the tips of the sled," Dash told her friends. "If we are going to pull the sled, we'll need to make sure the blades are smooth enough to glide over the ground." Her wings fluttered and she shot up in the air. "This sled is going to be *so mint*!"

Raina knew her friends would come together to make this happen. "I'll stay here and keep Lyra comfortable," she said. "Dash, do you think we'll be able to get Lyra to the castle before Sun Dip?"

"Yes," she said, "I do." Then she smiled. "I'm not sure we'll win any races, but we can get Lyra there before dark."

The fairies all flew off to get their supplies. Before the sun reached the very top of the mountains, the fairies were back at Fruit Chew Meadow.

True to Dash's promise, she built a sled with all the materials her friends had gathered. Soon they had a sled large enough for a unicorn in the meadow.

Melli and Berry held up the licorice ropes.

"We braided them to make them stronger," Melli said.

"Sweet and strong," Dash said. "I should get you all to work on my next sled with me." She attached the frosted licorice blades to the sled and then stood back to admire the finished product. "Not bad," she said, checking over the sled. "I think we're about done."

Raina was feeding Lyra tiny bits of rainbow gummy chews when she heard Dash's news. Lyra's horn was still dull and the unicorn had not spoken or sung a word. Raina tried not to show her concern, but she was very worried.

"The sled is finished," Dash said.

The five fairies surrounded Lyra. They each took a piece of the blanket she was lying on and gently lifted the unicorn to the sled. Dash had done a great job of measuring the seat. The sled was perfect for Lyra.

"Sour sugars," Raina gasped. She pointed to Lyra's horn. Instead of being dull, the horn was now black. "We have to get her to Candy Castle right away!"

CHAPTER
7

A Sweet Ride

"Grab hold!" Raina instructed as she tossed the licorice ropes out to her friends.

The fairies worked together to pull the large sled through Fruit Chew Meadow. Each of them held on tight to the braided red licorice ropes and pulled with all her might. As they passed Red Licorice Lake, no one spoke a word. Each fairy was concentrating on pulling the sled—and getting the sick unicorn to the castle.

"Not much farther," Raina called over her shoulder. Glancing back at Lyra, she saw that the unicorn was resting comfortably on the sled. Only her horn made her seem different. Raina didn't have to look *that* fact up in the Fairy Code Book. A dull black horn was not a sign of a healthy unicorn.

"Dash, this sled is smooth as caramel," Melli said. "I can't believe we are pulling Lyra all the way to the castle."

"This is one smooth, sweet ride," Berry added.

Up ahead Raina saw the tall sugar cube walls of Candy Castle come into view. Never had Raina been so happy to see the pink-and-white sugarcoated castle! If anyone could save the unicorn, it was Princess Lolli.

As the fairies neared the front gate the castle guards came out to greet them. Quickly the guards took over and pulled Lyra through the gates into the Royal Gardens. They had been expecting the sick unicorn, and they were ready for her.

Princess Lolli came out to the garden. "I knew you would get Lyra here," she said to the fairies. She took a step back to admire the sled they had built. "This is extraordinary!"

"We all worked together," Raina spoke up. She turned to smile at Dash. "But this was Dash's design."

Dash blushed. "Sure as sugar, it helped to

have a Caramel, Gummy, Fruit, and Chocolate Fairy around," she said.

The fairy princess laughed. "Well done," she said. "And we are all so grateful." She waved her hand toward the large front door. "Come, let's get Lyra inside. We have a special vanilla bath waiting for her."

"Will she be all right?" Raina asked. She watched as the sled was pulled inside the castle. "Her horn has turned black," she said in a hushed voice.

Princess Lolli put her arm around Raina. "Yes, I saw that," she said gently. "I was worried that might happen. But now that Lyra is here, we'll be able to help her. The vanilla bath will get rid of any trace of salt." She smiled at Raina. "Lyra is going to be fine. Your getting her here quickly saved her."

Raina lowered her head. If only she had gotten to Fruit Chew Meadow earlier! She should have listened to Dash. If she had, they would have found Lyra sooner. And maybe the unicorn would not be this ill.

"Raina, this isn't your fault," Berry whispered in her ear. She came up beside her friend when she saw the worried look on Raina's face. "The important thing is that we got Lyra here to the castle. Now she can get help."

Hearing Berry say this to her made Raina feel worse. She should not have taken that nap after lunch. She and Dash could have been in the meadow to stop Mogu.

Dash flew over to Raina and gently pulled her away from the others. "Mogu stirred up trouble long before we got to Fruit Chew Meadow," she told her. "Berry is right. At least now Lyra is safe here at the castle."

"But I . . . ," Raina started to say. Tears gathered in her eyes.

Holding up her hand, Dash cut Raina off. "No one is more considerate of the animals in Sugar Valley than you," she said firmly. "Please don't be upset. If we're going to get Fruit Chew Meadow back to normal, we have to get Mogu out of there tonight. We can do it."

"Thank you, Dash," Raina said. She wiped away her tears and took a deep breath. "I guess

the important thing now is to find a way to keep that salty troll out of the meadow."

"And those Chuchies," Dash grumbled.

"How about we fix the fence first?" Melli called over to her friends. "We have leftover caramel from the sled already at the meadow. We can use that to patch up the hole."

"If this is Mogu's work," Raina said, "a fence won't keep him out. Fences don't keep trolls out." She sat down under a gummy tree in the Royal Gardens. "We need to find a way to trick Mogu—or at least teach him a lesson."

"I had a feeling she was going to say that," Dash said, smiling. She sat down next to Raina.

"He can't keep bringing salt into the meadow," Melli said. "You'd think that he'd notice the damage he's done to the flowers and Lyra."

"Mogu only cares about himself," Cocoa told her friends.

"Too bad we don't know another unicorn with a rainbow horn," joked Berry. "That would make Mogu jump."

Raina flew straight up in the air. Her wings were moving as fast as the thoughts in her head. "I know how we can trick that salty troll!" Raina shouted. "First I need to get something from Gummy Forest. I'll meet you all back at Fruit Chew Meadow at the end of Sun Dip."

Before her friends could ask any questions, Raina raced off to Gummy Forest. She hoped with all her heart that her plan to trick Mogu would work. She never wanted to see Lyra looking so sick again. And she had a few hours left to save Berry's birthday—and Valentine's Day!

CHAPTER 8

A Gummy Good Idea

Raina sped through Gummy Forest. The sun was heading quickly toward the top of the Frosted Mountains. She didn't have much time! Raina worked quickly and gathered all she needed for her plan. She had to get back to Fruit Chew Meadow before dark.

This has to trick Mogu, she thought. If she could

get Mogu and the Chuchies out of the meadow, the flowers would bounce back by morning and the meadow would be safe for Lyra. The fairies could celebrate Lyra's return—and Berry's birthday. This was a delicious plan!

The gummy cubs and bunnies watched Raina work. They were curious about what the Gummy Fairy was doing and crowded around her.

"Sweet sugar cubes!" Raina exclaimed. She looked over at the group of gummy animals. "What do you think?" A smile spread across her face as she held up her work.

The animals were not sure what Raina was creating, but they sensed it was exactly what she had set out to make.

"Oh, I hope this works," Raina said to the animals. She reached over to pet a blue gummy

bear on the head. "Be good, Blue Belle," she said. "Look after the others for me. I will be back soon."

When Raina arrived at Fruit Chew Meadow, the sky was a deep lavender with spots of pink swirls. Normally, Raina loved Sun Dip. She enjoyed talking to her friends, telling stories, and sampling the candy crops of the day. Only today Sun Dip was not about having fun. Today Sun Dip was about tricking a troll!

"Are you ready to teach Mogu a lesson?" Raina asked as she touched down next to her friends. They were all waiting near the berry cherry tree.

"Sure as sugar!" Berry replied.

"We mended the fence with hot caramel," Melli said. "Mogu will have a harder time getting into the meadow now."

Raina took her gummy creation out of her

bag. She held up the rainbow gummy unicorn horn proudly. "This should keep Mogu and the Chuchies out for a long, long time," she said.

Melli gasped. "Where'd you get that?"

"Is . . . is . . . is that Lyra's horn?" Dash asked. Her mouth hung open and her eyes were wide with disbelief.

"No, silly," Raina said. "It's a gummy cone from a pine gummy tree," she told her friends. She smiled slyly. "And then I added a little more gummy candy."

"Lickin' lollipops, Raina!" Berry exclaimed. "That looks just like Lyra's horn!"

Raina's wings fluttered. She blushed a little too. "I was hoping you'd say that," she admitted. "The real test is if Mogu and the Chuchies think this is really Lyra's horn."

"What are you planning?" Cocoa asked.

Leaning in toward her friends, Raina spoke softly. "I was thinking if we hid in the bushes and poked this horn out, Mogu would get spooked that Lyra is back." She raised her eyebrows. "What do you think?"

"Holy peppermint!" Dash burst out. "You are *so mint*, Raina."

Her friends all nodded in agreement.

"It's a gummy good idea!" Cocoa blurted out.

Raina was glad her friends thought her idea would work. She hoped the horn would fool Mogu and the Chuchies.

The five fairies crept along the hedges lining the edge of the meadow. They didn't have to wait long. Soon they saw Mogu and the Chuchies approaching the gate. As they got closer Raina felt her stomach flip-flop. Seeing Mogu in his clunky boots caked with salt made her so mad.

"Just look at him," Berry snarled. "He doesn't even care that the salt on his boots made Lyra sick."

Dash popped up in between Raina and Berry. "Maybe he didn't know?" she asked.

Raina watched the grumpy, greedy troll. His big belly hung over his pants, and his white hair stuck up in a ring around his huge head. "He doesn't seem very concerned about anyone but himself—and his tummy."

"Well, look at this!" Mogu grumbled. He stopped in front of the mended fence. "Seems someone fixed the fence." He stuck his chocolate-stained fingers into the caramel patch, which had not dried yet.

"Yummmm," he said, licking his finger. "Fresh caramel is *sooooooo* good."

Melli's face turned a bright cherry red. She bit her lip so she would keep quiet.

Raina hunched down low and rustled the leaves in the bushes. Now was the time to get this show started! She slipped the gummy horn onto a stick.

"Meeeeeeeeeeee, meeeeee!" the Chuchies shouted, jumping up and down on their short, skinny legs. Their furry, round yellow bodies shook as they jumped.

"Shhhh," snapped Mogu. He held his hand up to quiet the Chuchies. Looking around, he narrowed his eyes. "What was that?" he asked.

"Meeeeeeeee, meeeeee?" the Chuchies asked.

Raina rustled the bush branches again.

"Couldn't be," Mogu muttered. He pushed down on the caramel fence where the caramel was still soft, and he broke through.

Holding tight, Raina swayed the rainbow gummy pinecone around. Then she stuck the horn through the bush.

"Salty sticks!" Mogu exclaimed. "How can that be?" He rubbed his eyes. The light was fading fast. "She's back?"

Raina looked over at Berry. Now was her time to sing! Berry nodded and smiled at Raina.

"Gentle breeze and sweet light, flavors of the rainbow grow bright . . . ," Berry sang out.

Raina was impressed by how similar Berry sounded to Lyra. As she sang Raina moved the horn just as if Lyra was there. When Berry finished the song, Dash popped her head up over the bush.

"They're leaving!" Dash cried.

All the fairies peered over the bush. Raina couldn't believe her eyes. Mogu and the Chuchies were running away!

CHAPTER
9

Three Delicious Reasons

Are they really gone?" Raina asked. She squinted her eyes to see in the early evening dim light.

"Yes!" Dash cheered. "The gummy pinecone trick worked!"

"Raina, that was *choc-o-rific*!" Cocoa blurted out. "You fooled Mogu."

Melli fluttered her wings and lifted off the ground. "And I don't think he'll be coming back anytime soon," she added. "I didn't think that Mogu could move that fast."

"Oh, we have to let Lyra know," Berry said. "I can't wait to see the look on her face." She turned to Raina. "Thank you. On behalf of all the Fruit Fairies—and all Candy Fairies—thank you!"

"Do you want us to go with you?" Melli asked.

Berry shook her head. "No, I'll go," she told her friends. "I feel bad that I wasn't here earlier to help Lyra. I was at Lollipop Landing this morning, and I wish I had been here." She lowered her head and fingered her fruit-chew bracelet. "If I'd been here, I would have been able to stop Mogu, and Lyra wouldn't be so sick."

At that moment Raina realized that she wasn't the only one feeling responsible for Lyra's misfortune. When something so sour happened, everyone felt bad.

"You know," Raina said to her friend, "we all feel responsible. I was thinking that if I had come earlier to the meadow, I could have stopped Mogu too."

Berry looked up at Raina.

"Me too," Dash said.

"We were thinking the same thing," Melli said, pointing at herself and Cocoa.

"I guess the important thing is that we did get here," Raina told them. "Lyra is getting help and Mogu is gone."

A smile appeared on Berry's face. "You're right," she said. "Thank you." She sniffed a little.

"I'll see you tomorrow. Red Licorice Lake for Sun Dip?"

"It's a plan," Raina said, giving her friend a hug.

As Berry headed off to Candy Castle, Raina looked around at Dash, Cocoa, and Melli.

"I think Berry forgot that tomorrow is her birthday!" she said. "What do you think of having a surprise party in Fruit Chew Meadow?" Raina saw her friends grinning. "It will be a triply sweet celebration—a homecoming for Lyra, a birthday party for Berry, and a Valentine's Day surprise for all Candy Fairies."

"Berry will love the idea," Cocoa said.

"She deserves a supersweet surprise for her birthday," Melli added.

A sugar fly landed on Raina's shoulder. The envelope was from Princess Lolli.

Princess Lolli
Candy Castle
Sugar Valley
Candy Kingdom

Lyra is doing well.
She enjoyed her
vanilla bath, and her
horn is back to normal.
She is going to be fine.
Many thanks to you and
your friends,
Princess Lolli.

"This must be news about Lyra," Raina said, opening up the note. "Dash, could you hold up a mint stick so I can read this? I hope this is good news."

Dash held up a bright mint stick as the fairies huddled around Raina. They were anxious to hear the royal news.

"Lyra is doing well," Raina read. "She enjoyed

her vanilla bath, and her horn is back to normal. She is going to be fine. Many thanks to you and your friends, Princess Lolli."

"So mint!" Dash exclaimed. "Now we definitely need to plan a celebration."

Raina took out a notebook from her bag. "We don't have much time to pull this party together. So we'll have to be fast." She started making a list. "First we need to try to keep this a secret. Part of the fun will be surprising Berry."

"And Lyra," Cocoa added.

Tapping her pen on her note-book, Raina tried to think of all the ingredients for a good party. "First, we need to send out invites with the sugar flies. We'll

have to make sure to write Top Secret so no one tells Berry about the party."

Melli peered over Raina's shoulder to look at her list. "How are we ever going to pull this party together by Sun Dip tomorrow?"

"Wait, there's Fruli," Dash said, pointing to the far end of the meadow. "Maybe she can help out."

Fruli spotted the fairies under Dash's mint glow and came over to them. "Is Lyra feeling better?" she asked when she saw the fairies. "I heard from a sugar fly that you brought her to Candy Castle on a sled."

"Yes," Raina said. "She's feeling much better."

"And we just tricked Mogu, so he won't be tracking in salt near the meadow again," Dash told her. "At least, not for a long time."

Fruli smiled. "Oh, I am glad to hear that," she

said. She shuddered. "I've never met Mogu—and I don't want to!"

Raina shrugged. "Oh, he's not that bad," she said. "Just a little salty."

Stepping forward, Raina moved closer to Fruli. "Tomorrow is Berry's birthday," she told her. "We'd like to surprise Berry with a party and also welcome Lyra home. We don't have much time, and we could really use your help."

"How delicious! I would love to help!" Fruli exclaimed. "I didn't know Berry's birthday was on Valentine's Day. I'll have to make her a special heart valentine."

"How about helping with the decorations for the meadow?" Raina asked.

Fruli clapped her hands. "I could do that!" she said. "My aunt just gave me this fabulous

blueberry and cherry material from Meringue Island. We could use it as a tablecloth or something and then get some rainbow lollipops to stick around."

Raina knew she had just asked the right fairy for the job. With Fruli's great design taste, she was sure Fruit Chew Meadow would look *sugartacular* by tomorrow's Sun Dip.

"Sure as sugar, this meadow is going to look supersweet," Raina said. "It will be a sugarcoated celebration." She smiled at her friends. "Now we just have to keep the secret from Berry!"

10

A Sugarcoated Day

Raina was up the next morning bright and early. She had so much to do! Not only did she have to feed the animals in Gummy Forest, she had a party to plan!

She'd have to do all her work in the forest quickly and then head to Fruit Chew Meadow. Knowing that she wouldn't have time to fly back home, Raina decided to take her party clothes with her now. Racing around her room, Raina folded her clothes neatly into her backpack. Half of Sugar Valley was coming to Berry and Lyra's surprise party that evening. If everything was going to be finished by Sun Dip, she had to hurry.

Luckily, the gummy animals were well-behaved, and feeding time went well. Thankful that the animals were calm and listening to instructions, Raina gave each one a little extra flavoring. "After all," she told them, "today is a day to celebrate!"

As Raina was cleaning out the gummy bears' feeding log, Melli suddenly appeared before her. The Caramel Fairy's face was bright red, and even when she landed her wings didn't stop fluttering.

"Raina!" Melli gasped. "Oh, I'm so glad I found you here."

Raina dropped the log in the water. "Is Lyra all right?" Raina asked. "What's wrong? Did you hear something?" She eyed her friend's nervous expression.

Melli put her hand up and tried desperately to catch her breath. "Everything is fine," she said. "In fact, everything is more than fine." She smiled. "I'm just bursting to tell you the sweet news!"

"What?" Raina asked. She couldn't imagine what news Melli had for her.

"Guess who is coming to the party tonight?" Melli finally managed to say.

The guest list for the party had gotten so long that Raina had lost count of all the fairies invited. She shook her head. "I don't know," she said, playing along with Melli. "Who?"

"The Sugar Pops!" Melli shouted. Once she said the musical group's name, her wings started flapping again and she soared up to the sky. "Berry is going to flip!"

All the Candy Fairies loved the three brothers who made up the Sugar Pops. Chip, Char, and Carob were three of the most delicious singers. Their music was always at the top of the charts in Sugar Valley.

"That *is* sweet news!" Raina exclaimed. "How do you know? Are you sure?"

The Caramel Fairy nodded quickly. "I was at Candy Castle early this morning to make a delivery, and I saw Princess Lolli," Melli explained. "She told me that Lyra is going home later today and that she'd heard all about the plans for the surprise party." Melli grabbed Raina's hands and started to jump up and down. "And then she told me that Dash had sent a sugar fly to Carob Pop! She let him know about Lyra's being sick, Berry's birthday, and the Valentine's Day celebration. Carob sent her back a sugar fly! Can you believe it?"

Raina shook her head. She was in sugar shock!

"He said he wanted to come sing with Lyra tonight at Sun Dip to help the flowers," Melli continued. She stopped jumping and sank down onto the ground. "Isn't that just the sweetest thing ever?" she swooned.

"Sure as sugar," Raina said.

Melli helped Raina pick up the feeding log and carry it over to the edge of the water. Finally

Melli's wings slowed down, and she was able to breathe normally.

"Having the Sugar Pops sing at the party tonight will sweeten the whole night," Raina said. She grinned at Melli. "Dash found the perfect surprise for Berry."

"And everyone in Sugar Valley!" Melli added.

Raina stuck her hand out and pulled Melli up. "Now we really have to make sure the meadow is looking good," she said. "We're going to have a huge party!"

"I know!" Melli exclaimed. "That's why I had to come here and tell you!"

"And you're sure Berry doesn't know?" Raina asked.

Melli shook her head. "All the sugar flies and fairies know the party is a surprise." Melli grinned. "I have to make sure I don't see Berry today. I don't think I can keep the secret."

Raina rubbed her wet hands on her dress. "I know how you feel," she said. "I'm going to have to avoid Berry all day too! Fruli is going to be with her most of the day and promised to keep her away from the meadow."

"Yes, I heard," Melli said. "And they will escort Lyra back at Sun Dip, right?"

"That's the plan," Raina said. She held up her crossed fingers. "I hope all goes well. I want this to be an extra-special surprise for them both!"

Melli gave Raina a hug. She took off, and called over her shoulder, "I'll see you at Sun Dip!"

Raina stood for a moment, smiling. Their plans were coming together: Lyra was healthy, Berry was going to have a birthday surprise, and now the Sugar Pops were going to sing! This was turning out to be a sugarcoated Valentine's Day.

For Raina, the day was spent making candy for the party and organizing the decorations. She had a quick visit with Lyra at the castle and was happy to see her feeling well.

Back at the meadow, plans for the party were going perfectly. Fruli had dropped off the gorgeous Meringue Island material, and Raina, Cocoa, and Dash hung it as a curtain on the stage.

"For once I'm glad that Berry is always late," Dash said as she hung mint lights around the stage. "I hope we finish in time!"

"Everything looks great," Raina said happily as she took in the scene.

The meadow looked beautiful with the festive decorations, and the flowers were all standing up straight.

"We actually pulled this together!" Dash exclaimed.

"Here they come!" Cocoa shouted. "Places, everyone!"

The fairies all gathered around the stage while the Sugar Pops played. Raina could see the surprised expressions on Berry's and Lyra's faces as they got closer. When the two of them landed on the stage, everyone applauded.

Berry just gazed around the meadow with her mouth open.

"I don't think I've ever seen Berry speechless!" Raina said, giving her friend a tight squeeze. "Happy birthday!"

"I can't think of a sweeter surprise for my birthday *and* Valentine's Day," Berry said. "Thank you all so much." She turned to Raina, Dash, Melli, and Cocoa. "You did all this?"

"Yes," Raina said. "We all helped. Especially Fruli."

Raina handed Berry a present. She was so excited to give Berry her birthday gift. When Raina had visited Lyra earlier that day at Candy Castle, Lyra had told her about the flower she had grown especially for Berry.

"Oh, Raina!" Berry cried. "This is scrumptious!" She put the headband on her head. "I love the fruit-chew flower and all the sparkly gummies."

"I'm glad you like it," Raina said. "Happy birthday, Berry." She went over to Lyra and

stroked her long nose. "And welcome home, Lyra."

Lyra nuzzled Raina's hand. "Thank you," she sang out.

The fairies all exchanged cards and other treats. The whole kingdom was there to celebrate the festive day.

"This turned out to be the sweetest Valentine's Day surprise," Berry said to her friends. "Lyra is healthy, the meadow looks great, and the Sugar Pops are here!"

Raina looked over at Dash and smiled. "Sure as sugar!" she exclaimed happily.

The Sugar Pops played well past when the sun slid behind the Frosted Mountains. Everyone was having a deliciously sweet time.

"This was the best Valentine's Day ever!"

Berry exclaimed at the end of the night.

"And I got some great gifts too," Dash said, grinning.

"Who doesn't love Valentine's Day?" Cocoa added.

Melli and Raina laughed.

"We all got some sweet surprises," Raina said. "But the sweetest part is that we helped Lyra."

"Look at Lyra now," Dash said, smiling.

Lyra was in the meadow, away from the crowds. She was softly singing her special lullaby to the flowers.

"Do you think she liked the party?" Raina asked.

"Yes," Berry said, hugging Raina. "And she loves being back safe and sound, surrounded by all these friends."

Raina smiled. This *was* a grand birthday and Valentine's Day event. There was no better way to celebrate Berry's birthday and Lyra's homecoming. They had tricked Mogu once again, and the Sugar Pops were playing. The sounds coming from the meadow were joyous and sweet. It was a perfect Candy Fairy celebration full of love and friendship!

Bubble Gum
Rescue

Early in the morning, Melli the Caramel Fairy flew to the top of Caramel Hills. She was checking on the caramel chocolate rolls she had made with her Chocolate Fairy friend Cocoa. Melli smiled at their newest creation drying in the cool shade of a caramel tree. Yesterday the two fairies had worked hard rolling small logs of caramel and then dipping them in chocolate. The final touch was a drizzle of butterscotch on top. Melli couldn't wait to taste one!

A caramel turtle jutted his head out of his shell and smelled the fresh candy. Melli laughed. "You were hiding over by that log," she said to the turtle. She kneeled down next to him. "Did you think you'd snatch a candy without my noticing?"

The turtle quickly slipped his head back into his shell. Still as a rock, he waited to see what the Caramel Fairy would do.

Melli placed one of the candies in front of him. "Of course you may have one," she said sweetly. "There's enough to share."

The turtle stuck his head out again and gobbled it up.

"Do you like the candy?" Melli asked.

The turtle nodded, and Melli smiled. "Cocoa and I are going to bring these to Sun Dip this evening," she said.

Sun Dip was the time at the end of the day when the sun set behind the Frosted Mountains and the Candy Fairies relaxed. Melli loved visiting with her friends and catching up on everyone's activities. And today she and Cocoa would bring their new candy. She hoped her friends would enjoy the sweet treat.

Just as Melli was putting the candies in her basket, she heard a squeal. It sounded like an animal in trouble. She put the basket down and walked toward the sound.

"Hot caramel!" Melli cried as she peered around one of the caramel trees.

Lying on the ground was a small caramella bird. He was trying to flap his wings to fly, but they were barely moving. Melli leaned in closer and noticed that the bird's feathers were wet and stuck together.

Melli reached out to the bird. "You poor thing," she whispered. She tried to calm the little one by talking to him. Caramella birds lived in the valley of Caramel Hills and had bright yellow wing feathers. They lived off the seeds of the caramel trees and filled the hills with their soft chirps.

"Where have you been playing?" Melli asked sweetly. She carefully picked up the bird and gently stroked his head. Immediately she realized that his feathers were covered in thick butterscotch. "How did you get coated in this syrup?" she asked. "No wonder you can't move or fly."

The bird chirped loudly. It was shaking in her hands.

"Butterscotch is not the best thing for feathers," Melli said, smiling at the tiny caramella. "Don't worry, sweetie," she added softly. "Let's give you a good bath and get this mess off your wings. I know all about sticky caramel." She patted the bird's head gently. "I will get you cleaned up in no time. Let's go to the water well and rinse you off."

Melli held on to the bird and flew to the edge of Caramel Hills. The tiny creature seemed to relax in Melli's hands, but his heart was still pounding. At the well Melli began to wash the butterscotch off the bird's wings. She knew she'd have to spend some time scrubbing. She had gotten caramel on her clothes before, and it often took a while to get all the goo off.

After a few rinses Melli began to see his brightly colored feathers.

"There, that does it," she said, feeling satisfied. She stood back and looked at the little bird. "You do have gorgeous yellow wings!"

The bird shook the water off his wings. He was happy to be able to move them freely. He bowed his head to Melli, thanking her for helping him.

"You should be able to fly now," Melli said. "Be careful, and stay away from the sticky stuff!"

"Hi, Melli!" Cocoa appeared next to her. "What are you doing here?"

"Cocoa," Melli gasped. "You scared me!

I didn't see you there." She pointed to the caramella bird. "Look who I found. He was covered in butterscotch, and his wings were stuck together. I just gave him a bath with the fresh well water."

Cocoa's wings fluttered. "Oh, bittersweet chocolate," she said sadly. "This is worse than I thought."

"What are you talking about?" Melli asked. "He's all clean now. He'll be able to fly."

"It's not only this bird I am worried about," Cocoa said. "I heard from a sugar fly that there was a butterscotch syrup spill on the eastern side of Butterscotch Volcano. That must be where this one got syrup on his wings. *All* the caramella birds are in danger!"

"Oh no," Melli said. "So many caramella birds

live over there. What else did the sugar fly tell you?"

"That was all," Cocoa replied.

Sugar flies passed information around Sugar Valley. If a fairy wanted to get the word out about something important, the sugar flies were the ones to spread the news. "Let's go now," Melli said urgently. "If Butterscotch Volcano erupts, there'll be a large spill in the hills." She looked down at the bird. "Is that what happened to you? Will you take us to where you got butterscotch on your wings?"

The bird took flight, and Melli and Cocoa trailed after him. His yellow feathers gleamed in the sunlight. Melli beat her wings faster. She was very concerned about what kind of sticky mess they were going to find.

Fly over
to meet the
Candy Fairies at

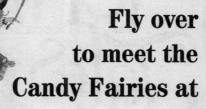

CandyFairies.com

See what the Fairies left behind:

- A sweet eCard to send to your friends
- *Choc-o-rific* activities
- Delicious recipes

**All you need to know about
your favorite characters!**

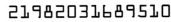

from "stilted 'primitive' English used in place of articulate Salish," and that some of the language used is "offensive to Indian people."

The agency was often visited by officials, the military, and writers, including Elizabeth Custer more than once. The whitewashed buildings, the reputation of Mollie's hospitality, and the history of peaceful interactions made the agency a showcase.

The conflicts with white settlers encroaching and the challenges of managing a large organization while working respectfully with three separate tribes are also documented. Peter did get the lake named Lake Mary Ronan, which is how it is listed on present-day maps. It is part of Lake Mary Ronan State Park. The mountain peak he affectionately referred to as "Finerty's Wart" was officially named for Peter and is known today as Mt. Ronan. I tried to discover how the Native people might have felt about the naming of the mountain and the lake after the Rona Uncertain, I gave Mollie pause in accept Peter's "gift," as I think that out of respect the Flathead people, she would have h least a moment's hesitation with the s commission's naming of Big Mountain L her.

There is also a town named Ronan an named Arlee and Charlo, based on the leaders of the 1800s. A 2021 nonfic about the Arlee Warriors basketball team of Arlee, Montana, by *New York Times* writer Abe Streep, offers a contemporary reflection on descendants of people Mollie and Peter might have known. Titled *Brothers on Three: A True Story of Family, Resistance, and Hope on a Reservation in Montana*, it followed the 2017 state championship team members and their community struggles and triumphs. It was serendipitous to have discovered the book before I'd finished my manuscript.

St. Ignatius, also on Montana maps, was one of the earliest missions in the West and is listed on the National Register of Historic Places. Following a fire in 1919, little of the community remains, but the brick church still stands with ˙e Mission Mountains towering behind it. The ˙ˑbishop did present a mass there, and Mollie ˙ s of an earlier one held in the mill at the ˙gency as well.

˙r's death, his clerk, Joseph P. Carter, ˙ted interim agent. Carter and Mary ˙ Hair—married in 1895, and Mollie ˙ children continued to live at ˙ few more years. When Carter ˙ full term, Vincent became the

˙ved to Missoula, Montana, ˙rsity, she wrote, so that ˙ might one day attend. She

432

spent the remainder of her life in Missoula. Her house on Pine Street still stands.

Peter did remove the little gold ring, Mary reports in her memoir. He let one of his girls play with it . . . and it was lost. But she still had the memory; those can never be lost.

In an epilogue of her memoir, Mary writes that her greatest joys in life came as wife and mother. "In their suffering, failures, and sorrows I have felt anguish unutterable, not to have been endured but for the faith that through our many tribulations we enter into the kingdom of God." I found Mollie to be a remarkable woman of faith and fortitude, and it's my hope that you, dear reader, do as well. She died in 1940 and is buried next to Peter in St. Mary's Cemetery in Missoula.

Acknowledgments

Thanks go to the Bitterroot Salish, Upper Pend d'Oreille, and the Kootenai tribes—also known as the Confederated Salish and Kootenai Tribes of the Flathead Nation—for preserving their history and culture and to their extensive materials available online. Writing during a time of COVID prevented travel, so I relied heavily on Mary's memoir, books about Montana, and online resources. Of special note is the official website of the Confederated Salish and Kootenai Tribes (www.csktribes.org), the Kootenai Culture Committee, and the Selis Qlispe Culture Committee Elders Cultural Advisory Council, who work to preserve and shape the direction of the stories told of tribal people. The Three Chiefs Cultural Center (threechiefs.org), formerly the People's Center, allows access to the story of this confederation of tribes as told through "a museum, an exhibit gallery, educational programs and a quality giftshop." In a temporary setting at St. Ignatius, Montana, it has now reopened for visitors. Nine Pipes Museum (ninepipesmuseum.org) at Charlo is an equally important museum that tells the history of the reservation but also that of the Jocko Agency—where the Ronans lived—specifically.

I tried to stay true to the stories as told through Mollie's eyes as relayed in her memoir. This included her spellings of Salish and Kootenai and Pend d'Oreille words and her remembrance of events such as the gifts of names, the visits by the archbishop, blind Michel, and the offers of protection during the Nez Perce War. It would not surprise me if her memory at times conflicts with the Flathead Nation's perspectives, though I found no evidence of such. I tried to be sensitive to contemporary understandings as well as honoring the story of this woman and her husband who spent seventeen years of their lives in service—which is how they saw their work—to the Native people they were allowed to live among.

Gratitude for individuals who assisted me goes especially to Ellen Baumler, editor of Mollie's memoir and my source book. And to Cary Heskett of Kalispell, Montana, who came into my life through her daughter Hilary whom we had the pleasure of hosting for several months some years ago while she served a physical therapy internship for her doctorate. Mollie's story was in the back of my mind then, and when I told Hilary, she told her mom, who caught my enthusiasm and to whom we are also now connected for life. Such are the ways stories bring us gifts. Cary connected with genealogists, contacted people from the Family History Center, gleaning information shared with her and ultimately with me. Cary also read a version of this book and helped correct and direct me toward making it an authentic Montana story. Research can be a spiderweb of connections. Hilary Heskett, through a friend, put me in touch with John Fraley, author of *Rangers, Trappers, and Trailblazers* and *A Woman's Way West, In and Around Glacier National Park from 1925 to 1990*. In a phone conversation, he graciously shared wisdom of his forty years with the Montana Wildlife Agency. Another researcher to whom I'm indebted is CarolAnne Tsai of Portland, who first provided me with connections about Mary Catherine Fitzgibbon Sheehan Ronan and who continues to be a support for writing whatever subject claims me. I'm also grateful to my friend Laurie Koski, who grew up in Fort Benton, Montana, and who now lives in Bend, Oregon. She graciously answered questions and told me how to pronounce the Ronan name (Row-NAN).

A number of books about Montana served me well. *Montana* by Clark C. Spence; *F. Jay Haynes, Photographer*, published by the Montana Historical Society; *The Last Best Place, A Montana Anthology*, edited by William Kittredge and Annick Smith; *Montana Women Homesteaders: A Field of One's Own*, edited by Sarah Carter; *This House of Sky* by Ivan Doig; and the volumes of Peter's agency reports detailing issues about payroll delays, recruitment challenges, ranching, even the whitewash packaging efforts. Despite the wisdom of these writers and these researchers, mistakes can be made, and they belong to me.

Especially helpful for understanding Mollie's life and her relationship with her father is the book *The AfterGrief: Finding Your Way Along the Long Arc of Loss* by Hope Edelman. Through the author's research and insights, I gained understanding about Mollie's loss of her mother at an early age and the separations from her father and how those may have affected her as both a child and an adult—and how loss affects us all, each in unique ways.

Thanks are in order for my pre–copyediting friend Janet Meranda who catches so many details while I can still correct them; to Revell editor Andrea Doering who always makes the stories better bringing wisdom and insight; to Barb Barnes who finds the mistakes I overlook and who wins diplomatic awards for how she tells me about them. Thank you to the full team at Revell—Michele Misiak, Karen Steele, and to the fabulous sales team. To Leah Apineru of Colorado who left the publicity business but who still does social media stuff for me, and to Anji Verlaque, my webmaster, much gratitude. Thank you tons! To many others who bring these stories to readers through Baker Publishing Group and to my agent of thirty years, Joyce Hart of Hartline Literary: I couldn't have done it without you. Thank you.

I extend gratitude to my prayer team, to my family who put up with me, and especially to Jerry who offers careful comments as I read early drafts out loud to him. I hope to discover errors and to make corrections to the rhythm, tasks that seem only to be found in reading from paper and out loud. He never falls asleep, for which I'm eternally grateful.

Last, and perhaps deepest gratitude, goes to readers for making room in your lives for these stories.

Of special note are the librarians, museum staff, and bookstore fairy godmothers who have carried my titles, many all forty of them, hand sold them, and spread the word. Thank you. Of special note:

Paulina Springs Books, Sisters, OR

Sunriver Books and Music, Sunriver, OR

Klindt's Books, The Dalles, OR (the oldest bookstore in Oregon)

Deschutes County Library, Bend, OR

. . . And Books Too, Clarkston, WA

Wacoma Books, Hood River, OR

Powell's Books, Beaverton, OR

Chaparral Books, Portland, OR

The High Desert Museum Gift Shop, Bend, OR
Hood River Historical Museum, Hood River, OR
Walla Walla Library, Walla Walla, WA
Aurora Colony Museum, Aurora, OR
The Pacific Northwest Booksellers

And the Sherman County Museum of Moro, Oregon, county population 1800, where I held my first book signing in 1991, and we sold out all 75 copies they'd ordered in.

If not already, please consider joining my Story Sparks newsletter at www.jkbooks.com, which I hope brings monthly inspiration into your lives as your many responses to it bring joy to mine. I am thankful to many more unnamed people who continue to walk beside me on this journey, writing stories that inform and strengthen my own faith and I hope do yours as well.

Warmly, Jane

Book Group
Discussion Questions

1. Did Mollie honor her mother and father? How did she do that or where did she fail?

2. Why did fairy tales appeal to Mollie? How do such childhood stories help define us? Do you have a favorite fairy tale?

3. Mollie spoke of memorizing Chief Black Hawk's speech. What did she gain by reciting his speech or Shakespeare's sonnets for people eating at the establishment? How did her wish to be dutiful—as Chief Black Hawk spoke of doing his duty—affect Mollie's decision-making?

4. Was James Sheehan a good father? Why or why not? Was Mollie a good daughter? Why or why not?

5. Mollie says she was a shy child, so shy she was afraid to ask her father what to call her stepmother. How did grieving the loss of her mother affect her shyness? How did

confusion by the absences of her father and being left with others affect her confidence?

6. How did Peter's absences during their marriage (at the mine, his political travel, supply missions to Missoula, etc.) differ from Mollie's father's absences? Or did she tell herself different stories?

7. What gifts of Mollie's gave her the most confidence? Her faith? Her facility with languages? Her love for Peter and her children? Her ability to anticipate another's needs and attempt to meet them? Her trust in the promise of the "storehouse of riches"? Others?

8. What are your gifts? What's in your storehouse of riches?

9. How would you describe the relationship between Mollie and Shows No Anger? Were they employer/employee? Friends? What events played a role in the changing of those relationships? Have you ever walked the path that transcended employer/employee into a friendship? How did that happen?

10. How would you characterize the stepparenting of Anne? Did she make the best decisions to

stay behind while James took Mollie to plays and on trips? What else might she have done to be the mother Mollie longed for?

11. Why did Captain George's mission to rescue his daughter so affect Mollie despite her being powerless to do much to bring about a positive resolution?

12. Did Mollie ever feel that she was enough in the eyes of her father?

13. How did Mollie's life as the wife of an agent encourage others? Or did it? How do everyday acts of kindness and bravery translate into blessings?

JANE KIRKPATRICK is the *New York Times* and CBA bestselling and award-winning author of forty books, including *Something Worth Doing*, *One More River to Cross*, *Everything She Didn't Say*, *All Together in One Place*, *A Light in the Wilderness*, *The Memory Weaver*, *This Road We Traveled*, and *A Sweetness to the Soul*, which won the prestigious Wrangler Award from the Western Heritage Center. Her works have won the WILLA Literary Award, the Carol Award for Historical Fiction, and the 2016 Will Rogers Gold Medallion Award, and have been short-listed for the Christy, Spur, and Oregon Book Awards. Jane divides her time between Central Oregon and California with her husband, Jerry, and Cavalier King Charles Spaniel, Caesar. Learn more at www.jkbooks.com.

Center Point Large Print
600 Brooks Road / PO Box 1
Thorndike, ME 04986-0001 USA

(207) 568-3717

US & Canada:
1 800 929-9108
www.centerpointlargeprint.com

PORTLAND PUBLIC LIBRARY SYSTEM
5 MONUMENT SQUARE
PORTLAND, ME 04101